Scent of the Hunt
Murder in Los Lobos

Black Hills Wolves Book 38

By
Cam Cassidy

Copyright © 2016 by Cam Cassidy
ISBN: 978-1-68361-014-4
Cover art by Fiona Jayde

Published by
Decadent Publishing Company, LLC

Look for us online at:
www.decadentpublishing.com

Murder in Los Lobos

After thirty-five plus books with over twenty authors, we have journeyed with the Tao pack as they returned from the brink of destruction thanks to the return of Drew Tao.

Drew's not the perfect Alpha, nor is he the perfect man, yet he remains committed to his pack and to making the Black Hills a fantastic place for them to live and thrive once more.

The four-book mini-series includes novels by Cara Carnes, Cam Cassidy, Rebecca Royce and Heather Long. Though each is designed to stand alone, they tell a cohesive tale that is enriched by reading them in order.

Book 1 – Scent of Murder
Book 2 – Scent of the Hunt
Book 3 – Scent of his Woman
Book 4 – Scent of Madness

We've seen changes in the pack, healing, and a rebirth hope and generosity of spirit. It is true that every journey faces a trial by fire, and this is the crucible, which will forever change the Black Hills Wolves. I invite you to join us as we rediscover what it means to be pack when murder comes to Los Lobos.

~A Note from the Author~

Thank you for joining in on the Murder in Los Lobos adventure. This has been such an exciting project for me not just writing the mini-series but being able to work with such great authors. It has been an honor. I have grown to love the entire Black Hills Wolves world, waiting as the rest of you for the next book. I hope you enjoy!

Please feel free to contact me anytime at AuthorCamCassidy@yahoo.com

Dedication

To all who stood beside me when things got rough. My Besties and Betas, Susie, Sonja, April, Margarita, Bernice, couldn't do it without you. My kids who put up with me spending hours in my writing loft eating mac and cheese... again, you are my heart

Chapter One

Hours before, Brogan Jones had traversed the rough terrain of the path leading to Los Lobos, his dark-black F250 truck navigating the rocks of the road—at least the pack called it a road. A more accurate description would be a wide animal track, cleared of the deadfall of trees. A trip home to meet up with Ryker, Thane, and Colt for a brief exercise then he would be back out in the world again. The town held too many memories, most of them bad. Too many temptations, ones he didn't deserve.

When he hit the final clearing, he stopped the truck. He shifted into park before he swung the door open. He hefted his large frame to stand and look out over the old town. It looked a damn sight better than it had when Magnum ruled as alpha. Drew and the Tao Pack had obviously been bustin' ass bringing the place back to life.

What a difference a day made. No preliminaries were needed; all four men knew each other and what to expect. The most accurate way to describe Ryker would be a man of few words, but, when he did speak, his tone commanded attention. Meetings and exercises around the town were nothing new. Keeping the town safe and secure from detection from outsiders was a job given the utmost priority. Boundary lines were in place, large rock formations and deep crevices created with the intent of keeping away unwanted visitors. The Tao were reclusive, and, now, thanks to Drew, again proud of their self-sufficient ways.

They had taken only a few steps toward the forest when screams rent the air, the hackles rising on Brogan's neck. For a brief moment, memories of the past, Magnum's rule of torture, the murder of his friends and family, flashed through his mind. Ryker let loose a low growl, immediately turning toward the sound. Brogan, Thane, and Colt close behind, ran toward the old barn, the site of some of Magnum's most heinous crimes against the pack. A place where, no matter how much the pack worked to repair it, or how many coats of paint were applied, the horrors still remained.

Brogan clenched his fists in barely controlled rage as they approached the scene. Drew lay on the ground, bracketed by members of the pack—a doctor and a healer from the looks of things. They would take care of him. Brogan could do nothing to help him. Surveying the scene, he studied the female dead on the snow. Sonya? Sandra? Something—he didn't know her name. She lay on her side, arms folded to cushion her head as though asleep. The odd bend of her neck revealed her permanent slumber. Her slender neck had been snapped. The frail human would have had no chance. Turning away from the scene, he inhaled deeply, closed his eyes, and let the let his senses tell him their story.

Scent.... One of the few senses with the ability to

take you back, transport you to a different time or place. Sometimes to a good place, others to one you would rather forget, or, more often in his case, a place you tried to forget but your mind refused to let go. His lungs filled with all the scents of home.

He turned slightly and inhaled. Sharp and spicy pine. A scent which brought back memories of a childhood long forgotten. Games played that made a young boy into the man he was today. Another scent caught on the breeze. Earthy, musky. The moss he knew could be found near the forest floor, covering the rocks and boulders never touched by the light of the sun.

Scent.... Pungent. He would have laughed at the scent under different circumstances. Only one place in Los Lobos offered it up. Gee's diner and his damn fried pickles. Nothing reminded him more of home than that specific scent. He scrubbed a hand down his face, catching the next one as the breeze shifted a bit.

Scent.... Sweet, fresh. "Fuckin' wildflowers," he murmured to himself. As always, he could be anywhere in the world and the scent brought a specific image to his mind. Sometimes it felt more like a damn vision quest he refused to take. For years, he'd tried to forget the image and failed. It didn't live in his mind; it had been burned into his soul. Hazel eyes, tipped-up nose, hair as dark as the midnight sky. One thought of Natalie Ann Gabbin, or Gabby as most of the pack called her, caused his chest to tighten. His alpha lay *near* death, and yet the thought of her caused his jeans to tighten and his heartbeat to grow stronger. He was kidding himself. The damn thing beat a rhythm more powerful than any shaman's drum. He groaned and pressed the heel of

3

his hand against the growing tightness. He could waste his time and come up with reasons he didn't live with his pack. When, in truth, it only took one word: Gabby. He groaned on the exhale and discovered, much to his relief, the wind had changed. Unfortunately, now the breeze told a new tale. One no longer belonging here.

Scent.... Heady, metallic. One that caused the hair on the nape of his neck to stand on end. The scent of blood...Drew's blood. Whose blood wasn't even a question that needed to be asked; any member of the Tao pack would know it was the blood of the alpha.

At one final scent, his body tensed, on alert. Fetid, repulsive. It clogged his throat, threatening to choke him. It seemed to seep into his soul and refuse to leave. The scent of death.

Ryker growled out an order with unadulterated rage. "Secure the perimeter. No one leaves pack land."

Murmurs of shock rippled through the members of the pack, the same phrase echoed over and over. "Drew's been shot."

He hadn't needed to hear the words. He felt them, as did every member of the pack. Each would remember the moment the bullet took their alpha down. Brogan forced back any worry. Drew was tough as hell. He'd fought his old man, Magnum, for control of the pack and sent the bastard straight to Hell where he belonged. Of course, Drew wasn't invincible, but Brogan prayed it would take more than a bullet to bring the big wolf down. Fear for the survival of the pack wasn't even a thought. Ryker would step up; the pack would survive and thrive under his command. But, the loss of Drew...he couldn't process even the thought and pushed it out of his mind.

Brogan joined Ryker, Thane, and Colt as Gee arrived. The old bear would be feeling the same emotions as most as the pack; of course he would never let it show. The old bear even managed to keep his voice stoic when he spoke to Ryker. "They're looking to you for direction. Don't coddle. Not now with their alpha clinging to life."

"What do we know?" Ryker growled.

"Best we can tell, Drew came across Sonya's killer. Damn near bled out before the patrol came across the scene. Bastard shot him point-blank in the chest. Repeatedly."

A feral rumble rose from the enforcer when he glared at Thane, Brogan, and Colt. "Find the bastard and bring him to me. *Alive.*"

"Charles and Sonya were real loud earlier tonight, got into it right after the pack meeting. She stormed out, and he chased her. No one seems to know what the row was about, but his scent is all over her." Gee crossed his arms. "Hard to imagine anyone in the pack doing this."

"No one except Thane, Brogan, and Colt are above suspicion. They were with me when this went down," Ryker growled.

A new commotion began when Dani pushed her way through the gathered crowd. That wasn't his concern. Thane would handle the female. He had a job to do and a different female to worry about.

For a moment, he felt relief as he did a quick survey of the pack, which gathered not far from the scene. Gabby wasn't there. Why not? Constantly sticking her nose in where it didn't belong, it wasn't like her to not be in the crowd. His protective instincts regarding her raced through him. A fine tremor shivered up his spine at the thought she could be in trouble.

While in town, he planned to check in on Gabby. Something he would normally have others do for him. Being around the nosey little female always brought back memories and emotions he wanted no part of. This didn't mean she wasn't watched carefully. If she needed something, friends within the pack would let him know, and he would make sure she got it. If something broke, he would pay a member of the pack to fix it. He'd managed over the years to take care of her without Gabby being any the wiser. Explaining he was the one behind the good deeds and why simply wasn't going to happen.

Taking care of one another was the way of the pack. Years ago, Gabby had become the little sister to almost all of them. Brogan's thoughts were definitely not of a brotherly nature, though. His chest heated at the thought of her. To him, the female seemed to offer sweet salvation. But after all the shit he had handled for Magnum over the years, he didn't deserve salvation and refused to claim the potential offer. In the end, it didn't matter. While he hadn't claimed the female as his, he would make damn sure she was safe and had what she needed.

Chapter Two

There wasn't much of a difference between Los Lobos or any other town for the most part. Especially where the gossip and rumor mills were concerned. Every town had one place to sit around and catch up on the latest rumors and there was no better place in Los Lobos to find out the latest than sitting on a stool at Gee's bar. The pack seemed to divide, half going to the scene, and the other half waiting for news at Gee's. The place always managed to gather a crowd. But, today, finding a place to stand proved the ultimate challenge. When Gabby first entered, the tense vibe threatened to suffocate her.

Earlier that day, she'd been shopping and visiting with friends and had the same reaction. Walking down Main Street, she caught the scent of blood drifting on the wind from the old barn. She had no desire to go up to the scene. It would be better to imagine what happened than to see it with her own eyes. Fine hairs at the nape of her neck stood up, and her muscles twitched with the need to shift. Tamping down on her finely honed survival instinct instead of shifting and running for home had been nearly impossible, but she'd managed. When word reached her that Ryker wanted the pack to gather at the bar, relief, washed over her. The old barn held too many ghosts.

Since the word spread, Gee's place had been packed. The entire pack was in a state of shock. Sonya dead, Charles missing, and Drew shot. These things happened in cities, with humans or those nasty wolf packs she had heard about out West. Bad things had happened in Los Lobos. Memories of a past they all fought desperately to forget. The Tao Pack had more than their fair share of death and misery with Magnum as alpha. Under Drew, the new town and new pack had risen from the blood of those who'd died fighting for the unity they now had. She shivered at the memories she tried so hard to forget. She sometimes felt like a living, breathing reminder of the evil Magnum left behind. Only with the power and strength of the pack had she managed to reach a point in her life where she could forget. Of course, she hadn't, but those memories remained under emotional lock and key.

Settling onto a barstool, she wanted nothing more than a shot of tequila to calm her nerves. Before she could order anything, Gee placed a Coke in front of her.

"Clear mind, clear thoughts, clear actions."

She had a brief thought of arguing with the grumpy old bear despite knowing what a useless endeavor it would be. No ever talked Gee into anything. Instead, she smirked. "Strong tequila, strong will."

For a second, she thought she heard a low growl. Gee was never exactly what she would call fun, but today someone needed to place a sign on the door.

Don't Poke the Bear. His attitude, she completely understood. Gee had only entered the bar moments ago, probably having been up at the barn with Ryker and the others.

The temperature of the room changed as if suddenly being thrown into a hot sauna on a cold December day. The palpable tension kicked up to nearly intolerable levels. Trembling from the need to shift, she grabbed her Coke, turned from the bar, and found out exactly why everyone seemed ready to jump out of their skins. Ryker entered the room. Worse, he headed toward the bar, his lips twisted into a snarl. Getting out of his way became her number one priority. She skedaddled to find an empty chair. No way, no how did she want to cross his path.

Avoidance of all things Ryker was a way of life for her when the badass wolf appeared to be in a *good* mood. Ryker's moods were never easy to tell. The only difference anyone would see was a little less of a scowl on his face. Never had he been unpleasant to her; menace seemed to be a natural vibe he threw. One which screamed, "Piss me off and die." His anger pulsed through the air. Gabby clamped her jaw shut tight when he spoke. "All of you need to go home. When there is a change in Drew's status, you will get word. I'm not answering your questions. You don't need to sit here and wait or gossip. When I know, you'll know."

Busy checking out her shoelaces when he said the word gossip, she still felt his gaze on her. She should've been appalled. She should've harrumphed or at least stomped a foot. Of course, she didn't. So, maybe in the past she'd liked to spend time around town chit chatting with the others and getting the lowdown on what was going on. It wasn't like she was some busybody sticking her nose into everyone's business all the time. She had a strict policy of only getting involved if she could help. Wasn't her fault the folks around there seemed to need a lot of help.

Chairs ground across the hardwood floor, and glasses clinked against the tables as members of the pack got up to leave. She'd finish her Coke and let the crowd exit before she followed. Ryker's orders were clear. With the barely controlled rage rolling off him, no one in the pack would push him. But the nature of the wolf called to them to pace and plan at any potential threat.

Raising her glass, she chugged down her drink, hoping not to end up with brain freeze from the amount of ice Gee had given her. Instead, the air in the room grew thick. Warmth started in her chest, radiating through her before changing to a blast of heat .Her skin began to tingle in anticipation. *Holy. Shit.*

There was one person who could elicit that response from her. She watched Ryker as he walked away from the bar. Other members of the pack left, and she knew she should follow the others out the door. Instead, Gabby sat as if her feet were suddenly encased in concrete. The crowd cleared enough she could see where *he* stood. Her perusal started at Brogan's muck boots then rose to the faded jeans tucked into them. Letting her gaze travel higher to where the waist of those jeans rode low on his hips. Tight black tee stretched across his chest, highlighting the cords of muscles.

Her heart wasn't the only part of her which fluttered over the package. Her girly bits gave their approval. When she reached his face, she swore her heart would stop altogether. His long dark hair was pulled away from his face and tied at the nape of his neck, his jaw shadowed with a couple of days' growth giving him a rough and rugged look. Her palm itched to touch his face, to feel those whiskers. Hell, her thighs tingled for the same reason.

Brogan nodded to Ryker. Few words passed between the two men. If she had been paying attention, maybe she could have caught the words, but everything in her focused only on the fact that Brogan stood yards away. His approach lifted her from the lust-driven fog. She felt powerless to move at the same time his long, powerful legs ate the distance between them. Butterflies seemed to be doing gymnastics in her stomach when he came close enough to touch. He leaned down then caged Gabby into her chair with his beefy arms before he said, "Go. Home."

Okay, well, maybe not exactly the how-de-do she anticipated. Then again, he gave her more than she usually received when he came to town. Normally, his arrival and departure through Los Lobos were only a nagging ache in her chest. After it subsided, other members of the pack would mention he had been there. She stared at the wall of black heat in front of her, for once speechless. It had been years since he came close enough for her to touch. His scent wrapped around her like a warm blanket. Dampness gathered between her legs. She closed her eyes, allowing herself a second to enjoy the sensation.

She yipped as her neck tipped back with a tug of her ponytail; her eyes flew open to stare up at Brogan's face. His jaw set tight, his whiskey-colored eyes pulsed as they bored into hers. "Do not make me repeat myself. Ass. Home. Now," he growled.

Did he growl at me? Part of her immediately

wanted to obey. Once upon a time she would have probably done exactly what he wanted. She would have tucked her tail between her legs and run home like a good little she-wolf at his display of dominance. But, she wasn't that wolf. That was before he made the decision to leave her and Los Lobos behind. Even though her insides had turned to mush, his words had barely left his mouth when her brain kicked back into gear.

"Wait one stinkin' minute. *You* are not my alpha, and *you* are not my mate. That right there, buddy, means y*ou* have no right to boss me around. Remember, you weren't *up* for the job."

With a low warning growl, he leaned toward her. Possibly home was a safer place for her to spend the day. Today, words seemed to be the stick she used to poke the angry beasts. Unfortunately, his growl seemed to have an unexpected effect. Tiny sparks of excitement jolted through her, legs trembling at the smoldering look in his eyes. Her jaw clenched, lips tightened, and she gazed at him with defiance. She locked her knees and planted her feet. She wasn't sure if she had enough strength to stand her ground so close to him with her panties now dripping and a high probability of an orgasm if he gave her his harsh growl one more time.

Crapity crap crap crap! She started to lose the staring contest. Seriously, the man had beautiful eyes. There was another feature she remembered liking a heck of a lot more. Her gaze moved slowly down his face until it reached his lips. Perfect lips made for kissing. Memories assaulted her. Memories of how those lips felt pressed against hers. More, how he'd kissed her everywhere. Thinking of one particular spot she enjoyed immensely caused her to bite down on her lower lip. Still, a soft whimper slid past her lips. Brogan's nostrils flared and eyes darkened as his pupils dilated, evidence of his own desire. Lost in his eyes, she nearly jumped out of her skin at the sound of Ryker's voice bringing her thoughts back to the room.

"Gabby, home. Now."

There wasn't a bit of confusion in her mind with that voice. *That* was an order. Ryker's command, she wouldn't deny. The sound of his voice was like a bucket of ice water; more than enough to jerk her out of her lusty haze and back to the room. The rise of blush on her cheeks would be as impossible to hide as her aroused scent. For shit's sake, Drew was in critical condition, Sonya dead, Charles missing, and she had been ready to use Brogan as her personal jungle gym. Home was definitely the place to be.

Her eyes snapped to Ryker only for a brief glance before looking to his shoes. She knew enough not to maintain eye contact with him. Throwing down a challenge to Brogan was one thing; offering one to Ryker? Not something she planned to do in her lifetime. Gaze on Brogan, she said, "If you'll excuse me, *he* said I need to leave now. *He* has the right to issue orders."

Trying to play off any effect he had on her, she ignored Brogan's warning growl. Even though her steps stuttered when his fingers combed through her hair as she walked away from him. Before she made it through the door, Ryker's hand wrapped around her biceps, stopping her. She returned to her examination of her shoes as he spoke. "Gabby, be smart, be safe. Perhaps living alone isn't in your best interest right now. Think about it. I won't order you to leave your home, at least not yet, but I know the

13

pack would feel better if you did."

Not simply the weight of Ryker's words but the sheer number of them he strung together seemed to crush her. The enforcer, the silent soldier, a man of few words must be feeling the weight of the pack falling on his shoulders. "I'll consider it. The cabin is my home. I feel safe there. If something changes, I promise I'll go stay with Embry and Sarah."

He merely jerked his chin, released her arm, and she left without looking back. Not that she needed to. She could feel the heat of Brogan's gaze following her. Out on the street, few pack members lingered. Now wasn't the time to stop to chat. It wasn't until she cut through the path leading toward her cabin and hidden by the trees of the forest that she no longer felt his heat. Stomping her way down the path, she shivered at the emptiness taking its place. Gods, why did she have to see him? Maybe it was better when he blew through town and she didn't have to face him. Being avoided and ignored definitely won over being left with a hole in her chest.

Focus was what she needed. Brogan excelled at what he did; the wolf was practically a legend and one of the best trackers in the pack. She prayed not only for the pack, for justice for Sonya and Drew, but also for her own heart that he would find the culprit responsible quickly then leave. If he stayed too long, she wasn't sure her heart would survive watching him walk away.

Chapter Three

B rogan walked to the door to stand beside Ryker and watch as Gabby left. He could still feel the softness of her hair sliding through his fingers like fine silk when she walked away. Hell, he should have never touched her in the first place. He knew better; avoiding her had become a necessity.

The chemistry between them ignited like an inferno whenever they were in the same room. Her fucking scent—pure, sweet wildflowers when he first entered the diner. One look at each other, one touch, and it changed. Wildflowers mixed with the exotic scent of her arousal went straight to his dick. Her scent seemed to cling to him, his cock hard as steel, pulsing with need. He willed the damn thing to stand down. Gabby wasn't the reason he had come and neither was his dick. A quick in and out of town. Make sure all protective barriers were in place then leave. Things kept getting more complicated. "Thanks for sending her stubborn ass home."

Ryker looked at him, his eyes intense, or, he thought, more intense than normal. His jaw tensed as he spoke. "Gabby isn't my problem, and she wouldn't be yours, either, if you would've taken what was *yours* years ago. I don't have the time or inclination to deal with this Dear Abby shit. As you know, Drew is still critical. Sonya is dead. She and Charles had words at Gee's the night it happened, and Charles is MIA. Thane and Colt are already out in the field. Get on it. Anything you find is to be reported directly to me."

Brogan tried to remember a time Ryker displayed any emotion. At times he seemed to be struggling to control his rage. He and the new alpha had a lot of history. Madness had consumed their old alpha. Magnum extorted Brogan, forced him to use his skills as a tracker against defecting pack members. The threat to his family and friends too great to resist, Brogan carried out his orders.

Every time he'd returned, he felt as if another black mark inked its way into his soul. The one person who had it worse than he did was Ryker. The right hand of a madman, his duties often titled him an assassin. Times had changed; their world had changed. Ryker had even changed. Still a coldhearted son of a bitch, but when Saja came into his life, she managed to soothe the beast he had become. Yeah, the past wasn't a place he was particularly fond of visiting himself. Instead, he forced back the memories of the bad years and focused on the present.

"I'll be in touch."

The men separated, and Brogan headed on foot toward the old barn. The trail might be hours old, but it didn't matter. Something was always left behind. He normally would be able to catch the scent or find some tracks to guide him. His job was simple. He just had to stand back, look at the scene, and let it tell him the story.

Approaching the barn slowly, he studied the location. The crowd from earlier was gone. When he finally got close, he realized exactly what a complete cluster-fuck he had gotten himself into. No one was to blame. The scent of Drew's fresh blood still hung in the air. Of course, the alpha wasn't the one he needed to track. He needed the killer. There were too many scents mingling, swirling together. Despite the number of tracks, no real footprints were left on the dirt road, high winds from the north effectively erasing the path. As he leaned against the old barn, he concentrated on clearing his mind, and waited. *Talk to me.*

In his mind's eye, he could imagine the timeline of the murder and attack. Help would come; pack protectors would have arrived on the scene swiftly— the sound of a gunshot echoing through the woods. After a quick assessment, someone went for help, while another stayed with Drew. Protectors took positions on the perimeter to protect the fallen alpha. Others took off through the woods and along the paths to search for the assailant in hopes of a quick retribution. Members of the pack would have shown the moment they felt the pain of the alpha. Brogan cursed. With all the activity, he couldn't lock on to a particular scent. It was all a tangled mess of fear, sadness, anger, hatred, grief, and resolve.

Hopefully, only a few would venture into the woods. Anyone seeking escape after committing murder would most likely head for the woods. Beginning with one path, he made note of the others to backtrack as needed. At first, he followed grass and weeds depressed by heavy boots. His attacker had to be male from the size of the tracks. No paw prints indicated he hadn't shifted. Low-hanging branches were broken. Drew's attacker was tall, nearly six foot or more. He followed the signs and scent, stopping dead when the scent vanished. *What the fuck?*

There had been no rain to wash anything away. Without a sign to follow, he continued along the trail until it ended at a stream. Banks on both sides showed him nothing. *Impossible.* Backtracking up and down paths on each side of the barn for hours netted him not a damn thing. Had Charles killed his mate, Sonya, in a fit of rage then shot Drew? He found that idea hard to swallow. Mates were cherished and protected. Madness came in many forms, sometimes beginning slowly, other times the mind snapping like a brittle twig. The way the tracks zigzagged through the forest, madness was definitely something he wouldn't rule out.

Beginning again at the old barn, he took a long shot and sought the paths leading to the homes. His head snapped toward the sound of voices deeper in the forest. Unfortunately, the wind was at his back, denying him the scent from his distance. He growled at the thought of other members of the pack out searching. The last thing Brogan needed was wolves strolling through the forest fucking up his tracks. He would find them and send their asses packing.

Getting closer to the scene, the masculine voice came clearer, a voice he knew and knew well. A pissed off, volatile Colt. With any luck, he had caught up with the attacker and this could all be over. With a burst of speed, Brogan ran through the forest. The blood in his veins heated as he caught sight of Colt, his body itching to join in the fight to take in the attacker. The combination of scents caused his gut to twist. One male. One female. Brogan's wolf snapped and snarled in his head at Colt's aggressive stance toward the female. Not just any female.

My female.

Colt's voice rang out, "What the *hell* are you doing following me? Now is not the time for nosey little wolves to be out playing in the woods alone. Do you know what could happen to you alone in the woods, little wolf? Huh, Gabby? Little wolves can get very dead. Did you hear about Sonya? You wanna know what happened? You want a good look at her? We still have her body. I can show you firsthand."

Brogan jumped between them. It took everything he had not to shift and rip Colt's head off his fucking shoulders. Both males immediately dropped to a fighting stance. Neither had shifted, choosing to remain in their human form. As a human, Brogan had more restraint. As a wolf, he would rip Colt apart for even an assumed threat to what the wolf considered his. The only thing to stop the impending battle was his scent. Charcoal and fire, of anger, but something else. A sharp, spicy scent mixing with frustration and concern. Brogan's fists clenched at his side to keep from attacking. He had to be rational. Colt would never attack Gabby, or any female. The male wasn't wired that way. Volatile and intense, absolutely. Colt was one of the team Ryker had put in charge of the case. They were all together. Colt wasn't suspect.

A small part of him wondered if maybe scaring the shit out of Gabby would get her ass home where it belonged. Unfortunately, his wolf saw Colt's actions as a threat. The motivation behind it didn't mean shit. Claimed or not, she was his to protect, and no one would threaten or scare her. His back to his girl and his focus remaining on Drew's cousin, he growled, "That's enough, Colt. You're getting close to a line neither of us wants to cross. Go about your business. I'll take it from here."

Colt snarled back, "She's fucking following me. You got one shot, Brogan. Bring your bitch to heel before she ends up dead, or I'll find someone who will. Ryker will have no problem locking her down until the case is solved."

Gabby's voice pitched high, giving away her fear. The fear she would have been better off holding onto and keeping her mouth shut. "Hey! I may be a bitch, but I am *not* his bitch, and I do *not* need to heel. I was walking, heard something, and wondered what it was."

Brogan reached out and grabbed her arms, leaning down so they were eye to eye. "You heard a noise? Is that really your excuse? There's a killer on the loose, Sonya's dead, the alpha's critical, and you thought you would investigate?" Now he knew how Colt felt as Brogan struggled to rein in his own anger. There was absolutely no way to describe the female other than too damn nosey for her own good. He did his best to take a calm breath, but his words still came out as a growl. "Ryker ordered you home, Gabby."

She snapped back, "Again, it's not any of your concern, but I *did* go home and remained there for hours before I came back out. In case you don't remember, I'm not even one hundred yards from my cabin. I needed to gather some kindling for a fire. I stayed in town longer than I thought I would. The dang woodstove went out, and I needed some hot water."

He leaned into her, nose to nose with the stubborn female. His jaw ached, clenched in frustration, and the nerve in his cheek twitched. He'd had enough. "Now would be a good time to be quiet."

"*You* can't, and absolutely *he* can't tell me what to do," she yelled, pointing first at Colt then him.

"You done? Yep, you're done." It didn't matter to Brogan. He was finished listening. He lowered his shoulder to her waist and lifted her. With a chin lifted to Colt, he carried her toward her cabin. Three steps was all it took to realize the flaw in his plan. Inches away from his face rested the sweetest ass he had ever seen. Her scent wrapped around him, filling his lungs with every breath. Fight and bitch all she wanted, one thing she couldn't hide from him: the scent of her arousal. Pure lust scorched through him.

Struggling, her legs kicking, hands pounding on his back, she screamed, "Cut the caveman crap and put me down! You have no right to carry me off anywhere!"

Crack! His palm stung from the force of his swat on her ass, but it had its desired effect. She let out a yip, but at least she kept her mouth shut and stopped fighting him. While it had the desired effect of quieting and calming her, the effect on him was anything but calming. Wild heat began in his chest and quickly spread through him. He wondered if Colt had been right about one thing. Maybe it *was* time to make Gabby heel.

Chapter Four

For the second time in one day, Gabby remained speechless. Being a witness to Colt and his explosive temper, or anyone's temper, as far as that went, had a tendency to temporarily halt her ability to speak. But it didn't mean she would allow Brogan to manhandle her and treat her like a child. Her backside still stung from his hand. Therein lay the problem. After the initial shock and pain had subsided, the tingles moved to an entirely different place. Once they neared her cabin, she renewed her struggle with him, wanting down. "You made your point. I'm home. Now, put me down."

His hold on her only tightened, his voice rough. "Not on your life, Gabby. I'm not letting go. If I have to cuff you to the damn bed, you will be where I know you're safe."

A tremor raced through her at the low timbre of his voice that seemed to settle and make itself at home between her thighs. Confusion clouded her mind. One part of her brain screamed *yippee* and did mental cartwheels. The other half wondered who the hell the wolf was carrying her through the woods like a sack of feed and what happened to the *real* Brogan. "You...you're...what?"

When she attempted to twist to look at him, all she caught was a profile. Brogan's jaw held tense, and he refused to speak. She wondered if he was fighting an inner battle of his own. A blush scalded her cheeks when she lifted her head and found Sarah standing on the porch of the cabin she shared with her new mate, Gabby's friend and nearest neighbor, Embry. As if Gabby wasn't embarrassed enough, Embry approached Sarah from behind, and wrapped his arms around her waist. Contentment seemed to roll off the two of them.

Not until they reached the cabin did Brogan bend and deposit her feet on the steps. Gabby faced him, his whiskey-colored eyes darkened with desire. Her skin heated and flushed, and her panties were done for. She nearly growled at her body's lust-driven response. She'd been there, done that, as far as things went with her and Brogan. She wanted him. That wasn't a fact that she could deny or hide from him. A knot tightened in her stomach even before they reached the porch. "Umm, thanks for the lift. I...you...I can show myself in, and you can get back to tracking bad guys."

She nearly tripped when he took her by the arm and pulled her up the steps. "Trail is dead and, after the shit you pulled, I need a clear head. A couple of hours of rest will do me good. Then I can start fresh."

He opened the door and turned to her, his scowl firmly in place. "Not locked? What the *hell*, Gabby! You know better than to not lock your doors. Why the hell do you think I had locks put on the door? Let me explain, to use." He shook his beefy finger in her face as he growled, "Do not fucking move. I can promise your ass won't like the consequences if you do."

Confused, Gabby remained by the door as he walked through the small cabin. She had grown up in this section of the valley. Their family cabin had burned to the ground years ago. She had barely escaped. Afterward, her parents had decided they'd had enough of Magnum's tyranny and moved deeper into the mountains. Things in the pack had steadily deteriorated. In their fear, they'd somehow managed to anger Magnum, which sent them fleeing the pack. They were no different than a lot of the others. Her parents fled. Gabby had refused to go. She argued Los Lobos was her home, the only place she ever knew. Magnum left them alone, for the most part, and her friends were there. When she refused to go, she never dreamed they would leave without her. Even though she never said the words, they knew, everyone did. The pack wasn't the only reason she stayed. No matter how difficult things became with Magnum, leaving Los Lobos wasn't an option. Brogan may have come and gone back then on assignments for Magnum, but he was there. She could never call any place home that didn't include him.

Devastated and heartbroken when her parents left, she moved into one of the guest cabins. Their place hadn't been a mansion, but the cabins barely qualified as shacks. She did her best, members of the pack helping her out with blankets, pillows, and other things she needed.

Brogan had been away on an assignment for Magnum when it had all gone down. He had always kept his distance from her, but neither could deny the pull between them. She'd never regretted not leaving with her family. She would rather live with the hope of a future with Brogan than the thought of never seeing him again. He always used the same tired argument of her being *just* a pup. There were only eight years between them, so his argument never felt right. It made her feel unwanted by the only male she ever desired.

After finding out about the fire, Brogan became obsessed. He drew up the plans and, with the other members of the pack, helped to build her a new cabin. Benefits of pack life, everyone helped and looked out for each other. Her new cabin had been completed after living in one of the guest cabins for months. Her first night, she felt like a princess in a palace with Brogan her knight in shining armor. At least he played the part for a while.

Building the cabin, spending hours together only strengthened the desire between them. He gave her his friendship, he gave her a place to live, but, in reality, he gave her so much more. One unforgettable night. One night of every dream she ever had coming true before he walked away. There wasn't a doubt in her mind as far as Brogan was concerned. He was *her one* and she the same for him. When they came together, their bodies joined, the fates had aligned and offered them something so beautiful, so pure she thought her chest would burst at the depth of her love for him. They were true mates. She wanted it. She had thought Brogan did, too. In the end, he chose to walk away from her the very next day, leaving her heart crushed in the process.

Locking the memories away, she listened to the sounds of his boots on the hardwood floor. She rolled her eyes as he walked back into the living room. "You do realize I live in Los Lobos, not Los Angeles. Not a lot of breaking and entering here. I feel sorry for any wolf who would try something that stupid with Ryker

25

around. Los Lobos is safe."

Brogan reached around her and locked the door. She froze as he leaned down, the tip of his nose brushing hers and his breath warm and moist gliding teasingly along her jaw. "Not a lot of murders, either, but we just had one. I want the damn door locked, even when you're inside."

Fight him, kick or punch him, she shouted in her head. Instead, her wolf wanted to snuggle and melt against him. Her heart raced, and she hated the desperate tone of her voice when she spoke. "What are you doing here, Brogan?"

Tugging her from the wall, he closed his arms around her like steel bands as his lips hovered over hers. "Taking what's mine."

Chapter Five

Inside, his wolf howled. There would be no controlling it, no stopping it. They had been apart too long. The musky scent of her desire...putting herself in danger.... His primal need to keep her safe snapped into place like an iron rod. She was his, plain and simple. Despite everything going on, he needed to show her exactly what the term meant.

Tentative at first, he ran his tongue along the seam of her lips, and she opened. One taste and the kiss detonated. A fire of passion burned through him. He wanted to take his time, wanted to watch her strip bare for his eyes, and wanted to worship her body the way she deserved. He needed to gain some control, or it would be over before it started. Forehead pressed against forehead, he studied the hazel eyes he'd seen every night in his dreams. "Jesus. Fuck. I've missed you, Gabby.

She trembled against him. Flattening her palms on his chest, she pushed him. "You can't do this to me again, Brogan. It's too hard to watch you leave."

If she only knew how hard it had been for him to keep his distance from her, to deny the most primal force inside him. He'd learned to live with the pain, only eased by that distance between them. Within hours of being back around her, he was done for. One kiss and the burning pain in his chest completely disappeared; replaced by a contentment he had never known washing over him.

"Not walkin' away this time, baby." He leaned down and let his lips brush over hers. He wouldn't force himself on her; she needed to give him a sign. Never had the words felt as right as they did when he held her in his arms. "Gimme your mouth, baby." He got the sign he needed when she pressed her lips against his. He took over the kiss, dominating her as he slid his hands along her back to grasp the globes of her ass. Lifting her and deepening the kiss, he walked them to the bedroom. He stood her beside the bed and wasted no time divesting both of them of their clothes before pushing her down gently. Slowly, his gaze moved up her body.

"Better than my fuckin' memories. Jesus. Fuck. More beautiful than I remember." He leaned over her, cupped her cheek, and again took her mouth before moving her to sit at the edge of the bed. He pressed her back. He wrapped a hand around her ankle, kissing his way up to her thigh before he placed it on the bed then did the same to the other.

Kneeling on the floor in front of her, he slid his hands down the inside of her thighs and pressed out. "Spread for me, Gabby. Show me my pussy." He stroked his cock, watching her spread her legs. "Gotta taste you first, baby. Wanna hear you scream my name then I'm gonna fuck you." He felt the shiver race across her skin at his words, and grinned.

Her answer was a soft whimper. "I missed the way you touch me, Bro. Please, I need you."

"Fuck, so wet for me." With his tongue flat, licking bottom to top, he groaned at the first taste of her pussy, his cock twitching in appreciation. He buried his face in her sweet cunt and feasted like a man starved, tongue sliding through the folds, and wondered how the fuck he lived without her. He teased her clit with gentle nibbles and flicks with his tongue until her body quivered with need as he kept her on the edge.

"Please, Bro, please let me come."

He growled at the sound of her voice, husky and panting with need. A need he had every intention of filling. He inserted one finger then two and began fucking her, hooking them to hit the special spot deep inside her. "Love it, baby. Take what you need. Fuck my fingers. I want you to come on my hand. Now. Come for me, Nat."

Trembles became spasms, her pussy clamping down on. All it took was his teeth scraping over her clit before he sucked it into his mouth as she came apart, her cries of pleasure filling her room. "Brogan! Oh! Oh! God!"

Rising, he scooped up her still trembling form and settled her on his lap. He kissed her, letting her taste herself on his tongue. Her soft moans had sent tingles up his cock. Gods, he needed to be inside her. "What do you want, baby? Tell me."

"Your cock, please, Brogan. Give me your cock." He settled his hands on her waist then lifted her with every intention of slowly lowering her onto his engorged cock.

"Fuck. So tight. So fuckin' sweet." Her heat wrapped around him, his control holding by a fine thread, one she snapped easily when she wiggled, trying to force herself down on him. Grabbing her hips, he rose, at the same time pulling her down on him. Her soft moans and mewls of need grew drove his hunger. She writhed against him. His wolf growled in his head, wanting to mark her, wanting his scent forever on her skin. He lost control, his fingertips digging into her hips. He went wild, his blood like molten lava flowing through his veins as he took her hard.

Almost there. His balls tightened, and there was no going back. "Get there, Gabby. Come with me. Come now, baby."

He held her easily in one hand, the other slipping between them to flick her clit. She came wildly, thrashing in his arms, her pussy squeezing his cock. He buried his face in her neck and growled out his own release.

His tongue lapped at the sweet spot where her neck met her shoulder. Having his scent on her sated his wolf. Gods, he loved her, would move mountains, do anything for her happiness. His fangs ached to sink into her soft skin. To place his mark for everyone to see, to officially claim her as his mate. His canines elongated, and his tongue still lapped at the site. Lip curled, he prepared to mark her. The complete devastation on her face as she stood outside her ruined home filled his mind. It had been his fault. He should have been there, watching over her instead of tracking innocent members of the pack for Magnum. The memory hit him with such force, he pulled away. Instead of marking her, he kissed the sensitive skin. She deserved a better man. They were mates, something he knew in his very soul. The thought of her with another male nearly put him in a murderous rage, but he had to give her a way out if she ever wanted it.

Missing her almost immediately, he went to the bathroom, collected a washcloth then dampened it with cool water. At her side once more, he spread her legs and cleaned her gently. The lips of her pussy were red and swollen. He hadn't intended to take her that hard. After cleaning himself, he tossed the rag into the clothes hamper before gathering her up in his arms, her head resting on his chest, his fingers stroking through her hair. He needed to rest. He needed to get back out and on the trail. For now, more than he needed his next breath, he needed to hold her a while longer.

Plastered against Brogan's chest Gabby wasn't sure how long they lay there in the silence. Not that she didn't have things to say. She had plenty. Right then, she wanted to stay in the moment with him. Even if she did want to talk, she couldn't trust her voice. Emotionally, she felt too raw. There was only one person she had to blame, herself. All she'd needed to say was a simple no, but she hadn't. She had felt his teeth on her neck and allowed herself to have hope he would finally give them their dream. A mark on her neck to prove to everyone she was wanted. It turned out hope and joy were fleeting, fragile emotions shattering over his stupid male pride.

Untangling from him she turned away, pulling the covers up over her. She made not a sound as the first silent tear fell. Not wanting to think about the hurt, she tried to tell herself she'd had two really great orgasms to end a long dry spell.

Chapter Six

Sometimes, not only in town or in a crowd of people, you can hide. Sometimes a person can feel invisible. He stood hidden in the shelter of the trees watching a couple stand on the porch of the small cabin. It was a beautiful place, nestled in a grove of pines. It would be the perfect place to start a family. The perfect home. The wind blew and on it came the scent. Human, and along with it the pain. Why did there have to be so much pain? His fists clenched, his stomach knotted, and what felt like a lightning bolt shot through his head. "No, no humans!"

Humans were forbidden here. They made the town unsafe, the pack unprotected from the outside world. Humans were a danger. Not to mention, simply stated, it was plain wrong. Humans and wolves were not meant to mix. How many times had he heard the declaration in the past? His mind felt heavy. He reached up, his fingers sliding through the hair at the side of his head and pulling. Were they dreams? Visions? Memories? Had Magnum again escaped death and returned? He needed to get to town, to be with his pack. They would have the answers.

Sharp laughter drew his attention, and he lifted his face to the air, catching the scent. "Human," he snarled. *No!* he roared in his mind. It couldn't be her laughter. Was she mocking him? Had she come to use her human frailty to seduce her way into the pack before destroying it? Was it her laughter? Silently, through the forest, he followed the sound, not stopping until he saw them. Saw her. Head tossed back in laughter, long dark hair blowing in the breeze. A male accompanied her. Embry, his arms tight around her waist, pulling her toward him. Lunging away from him, she squealed, but Embry was too fast and caught her from behind, lifting her off the ground.

Her screams! Oh God, her screams. With the sound, his world turned black.

Chapter Seven

G abby's tears crushed him. She hadn't made a sound, but he could smell them, a salty ocean breeze filling the room. A deafening silence filled the cabin as Brogan got out of bed and dressed. He needed to get back out on the trail, or maybe it was an excuse. Another one of the reasons Gabby deserved better. A better man would stay in bed, hold her in his arms, and make gentle love to her. Not him. He glanced around at the home she had created. The cabin had been nothing more than a shell with meager belongings when he had been there last. The determined female had carved out a life for herself and made the place hers. No flowers or frills, each room rustic. Her furniture seemed to invite anyone who entered to sit, make themselves comfortable, and stay a while.

He needed to get back out and take care of the business that brought him back to Los Lobos in the first place. Gently, he tucked the blankets up around her, not wanting her to get a chill, and placed a soft, lingering kiss on her neck. He hadn't intended on waking her, the need to touch her too great. "Sorry, I didn't mean to wake you. I'm heading back out, locking up behind me. Stay safe." Quietly, he left the bedroom, closing the door behind him.

Fuck, he was torn. Two sides of him were fighting—one to stay with Gabby and the other to be out tracking. He'd been pissed off when she'd said she'd been out gathering wood the day before. It wasn't that he felt her incapable. Gabby had proven to be one of the strongest females he knew. It pissed him off knowing he should be there so she didn't have to. *Double fuck.* He needed to get his head back in the game and track down the male who killed Sonya and shot Drew. He hated it, but dealing with Gabby would have to wait.

Walking through the forest, he let nature and the wind tell him the story. While there was no way to prevent his scent, his grandfather had taught him everything he knew. The fresh soil he gathered hung wrapped in burlap around his neck to help keep his scent down. He wore soft-soled boots made of Neoprene, which repelled scent, instead of leather. No shuffling of his feet. Each step planned, heel first, rolling to the ball of his foot. Finally, he'd tied an old piece of twine around each ankle, a small twig hanging in the back. Any noise he did make would be assumed to be from nothing more than a small animal.

Confusion and, he had to admit, a bit of anger set in after he had again combed through the forest for hours. He would catch a scent, only to have it disappear and, shortly after, a new one took its place. He would never give up. Letting down Drew, Ryker, or the pack wasn't an option. Guilt from the past seemed to rise up and threaten to choke him. Memories of the past. When Magnum had learned of a pack "defector" as he referred to them, Brogan had been charged with tracking them down and bringing them back. Over the years, he lost count of how many wolves he'd dragged home to face their deaths. At least the lucky ones faced death. Others were left to the torture of a madman.

Fuck! He couldn't lose his focus. His trail had brought him back nearly full circle. Up ahead, he could see the cabin of Sarah and Embry. He might not live in town, but that didn't mean he didn't keep up on everything which could have an effect on Gabby. Including her new neighbors. The female, Sarah, was the newest human to join them. Their cabins were close. While the pack camaraderie was definitely up, most built their homes a distance apart for times of solitude. As expected, their scent was the most prominent, and tracks led away from the cabin toward the stream. Two sets of tracks, close enough together, Brogan knew they had to have their arms wrapped around each other's waists. No doubt, the newlyweds couldn't keep their hands off each other even long enough to take a walk through the forest.

Brogan veered off the path he and Gabby had taken yesterday. An odd sensation assaulted him, a tingling in the base of his neck. Barely fifty yards from the path, a large pine tree caught his eye. Needles bent, tender branches broken. The overwhelming scent of pine was not surprising, but the scent was mixed with the scent of wolf, but not a wolf he recognized. Closing his eyes, he inhaled again, and the scent seemed to change. He scrubbed his hand down his face in frustration. The deep depressions, multiple tracks in one place, suggested the wolf had been there a while, but not why. He stepped into the position, his feet taking the place of the boot prints on the pine floor. Slowly, he looked around. The tingling sensation grew stronger as he realized there could only be one thing worth watching from this vantage point...Embry and Sarah's cabin.

Without thought, he shifted. Bones and muscles twisted and snapped into place. The wolf was his strongest form and felt the threat against the pack. With large strides, he quickly covered the ground to the porch of the cabin. It only took a few seconds to discern they weren't home. He heard no heartbeats; the scent felt cold. After leaping the railing, he tracked their path. The lovers' route took him past Gabby's place.

A primal growl echoed within him. *Mine.* Part of him wanted to stop, ensure his mate remained locked safely inside. Tamping down the need, he focused on his duty, His wolf only gave in, knowing he was protecting his mate and would be with her soon.

He had only gone another two hundred yards before his hackles rose. An unmistakable scent clogged the air.... Death.

Almost to the stream, he found Sarah. Like the others, she lay on her side as though sleeping. Shifting, he crouched and placed his fingers on her neck. The act was unnecessary; he had no doubt of her death. The wind had already told him the horrifying tale. He had seen her yesterday, her smile bright, eyes sparkling as she stood on the porch in Embry's loving embrace. Now she was dead, her skin cool to his touch, a bluish cast to her lips.

Brogan stepped back to look at the scene. Sarah's body had no visible signs of trauma, no blood. The position of her body on its side, her arms bent, hands placed together under her cheek, made it look as if she had laid down and fallen asleep. The odd angle of her head made it obvious that, the same as Sonya, her neck had been snapped. *What. The. Fuck!*

Distancing himself from the body, he took in the scene. Leaves scuffled. Two sets of tracks entering. One set leading away. The scents of both Embry and Sarah lingered in the air, accompanied by others. The same confusing scents he kept running into, ones laced with anger, sadness, even regret.

Dread filled him. Not only had they not yet found their killer, Sarah was dead. Where the hell was her mate? He briefly wished they had better cell service. The changes had helped, but it remained spotty in some areas. What he had to do would alert not only Ryker, but others in the pack. Quickly, he shifted to his wolf, let his head fall back, and let loose a mournful howl. Knowing Ryker, he would have been waiting for the sound of the call and come immediately. What he would find when he arrived, Brogan feared would push his friend closer to the limit.

Brogan shifted back. His hackles rose as he heard the responding howl carry through the forest. No one would misinterpret the angry, nearly feral quality they all knew could only come from Ryker. It wouldn't be long before the enforcer and men he trusted arrived. Brogan would use those few minutes to memorize the scene. He wouldn't leave until others came to take care of Sarah's body; he wouldn't leave her remains to be ravaged by wild animals. Crouched back down beside her, he moved her hair away from her neck, revealing the mottling beneath the skin. "Who the fuck would do this? Why?"

More unanswered questions to add to the ugly mystery. He snapped his head to the side at the sound of footsteps in the forest, voices growing closer, quickly closing the distance between them.

Only minutes had passed since his call with Ryker, too soon for it to be him or any of the pack protectors.

Three males of the pack, none he knew well enough to even know their names, none of whom would have been sent by Ryker, came toward him. Their anger pulsed as they approached. "What the hell? Sarah, man? Oh my fucking God! You killed Sarah. A helpless *human*. You get off killing humans...females! Stand up and get away from her."

Brogan stood, taking careful steps away from Sarah's body to protect the scene. "You boys got no business here. Head on back home. Ryker's on his way."

The male in the middle fisted his hands at his sides as he spoke. "And we're supposed to believe you? You may be a part of the pack, but you're more like a nomad, blowing in here whenever you feel like it. Kind of a big coincidence when people start dying and here you are. Not to mention, we come through and find you with your hands on the body. We'll take you down and serve your ass to Ryker ourselves."

Brogan kept his eyes on the male who spoke, the other two, apparently thinking they were invisible or some shit, moving slowly to try to position at his flanks. There wasn't a snowball's chance in Hell they could take him, even three on one. The problem was, the last thing Ryker needed right now was to deal with vigilante shit from them or Brogan killing the assholes for being stupid. With the latest discovery, he'd reached his own limit. Not in the mood for their shit, he fought to keep his wolf in check.

The one who appeared to be the leader shifted to a large gray wolf, snarled, then crouched low. From his stance, any moment the wolf would launch himself through the air and attack. The other two would follow. Brogan tilted his chin as he caught something in the air. His fan group was in for a surprise.

Timing being everything, the wolf launched itself. Brogan was ready to shift but waited. In his wolf form, Ryker collided with Brogan's would-be-attacker and sent him flying through the air to land in a whimpering heap. Ryker's hostile growl cowed the others, and they retreated slowly, gazes on their boots. When he looked toward Brogan then beyond to the body of Sarah on the ground, Ryker's rage seemed to vibrate over them all. He stared for several long, tense moments.

"No time for this shit, man. As much as these ass-wipes deserve for you to take a bite out of their asses, I need to get on the trail." Hands raised, Brogan kept his own anger under control as he spoke.

Ryker seemed to debate Brogan's words. An impressive feat, considering the enforcer preferred to be a man of action. The large wolf finally shifted back to human. "Pick him up. Go home and do not leave. If I see, hear, or even *think* you have defied me and left there, I will find you. I give you my word, you won't enjoy it." Though he didn't look at the boys, no one could mistake his orders.

Not since the old days, old ways had Brogan seen his friend so close to gone. He had locked it down, his face void of emotion as he walked over and bent to Sarah and murmured, "Another human."

"Looks like she and Embry came down here. Whoever is behind this is fucked up. I feel like I'm chasin' my tail, something that never happens to me. I catch a scent or trail to follow, and it just fuckin' disappears. Never ran into anything like it before."

Ryker stood, his emotional mask firmly in place,

and tilted his chin, the only acknowledgement he'd heard Brogan.

"Man, I did not say I'm giving up." The last thing Brogan planned to do. "We will get this fucker and he will pay for...."

Two things happened at once: a scream rent the air, and the wind shifted. Both turned the blood in Brogan's veins to ice. The scream of a woman, the scent on the breeze.... Gabby, blood, and death.

Chapter Eight

Stir crazy. Those were the only words Gabby could use to describe her state. Brogan had been in town for less than twenty-four hours, and the proverbial door to the past she held under lock and key had been blown to smithereens. It wasn't enough his scent filled the cabin. Every time she moved, her body ached in a deliciously wicked way, reminding her last night was more than a dream. It felt like her girly parts were starting a conga line while her heart played the death march.

Enough! Thinking all things Brogan started the walls closing in on her. Tired of being alone with her thoughts, she decided to head out. The day before, Ryker had sent everyone home, but so far today, there had been no news. Brogan would get his tail in a twist if she went outside, but he would get over it. He had been at Gee's when she told Ryker she would go to Sarah and Embry's place if she felt she needed to. She had mentioned she would go if she was scared to be alone, which wasn't exactly the case. She simply needed to not be alone, needed a conversation focused on something other than her own personal drama.

After she dressed in a simple peasant dress and flip-flops, she followed the path up toward Sarah and Embry's. Simply being outside in the fresh air helped her clear her head. Her focus shifted to listening to the sounds of the forest. Birds singing, squirrels barking in the trees. She kept a steady pace and reached the cabin in no time, climbed the stairs, and knocked on the door. Knocking again, she waited a few minutes but still no answer.

Sarah and Embry were newly mated. The idea that they were locked in each other's arms and passionately unaware of visitors wasn't that far-fetched. She should have thought before she interrupted them. Still, with everything going, they should have at least opened the door. Listening for a moment, she caught no sounds of movement or voices. Maybe they had gone into town. Town sounded perfect, everything she needed. People, voices, and Gee's fried pickles everyone knew were the cure-all for everything.

Leaving their porch, she angled toward the shortcut to town, the path familiar to her. She hadn't gone far when she caught the scent of Embry. Eager to catch up with him, she followed the scent. The last thing she wanted was another confrontation with Ryker or Brogan.

Her senses heightened when she veered off the path. A sense of unease slithered up her spine. The forest had gone eerily silent as she made her way down the valley. She had to twist and turn around the brush. Her mouth tasted of metal. There had to be a dead animal nearby. Disposing of it would be a perfect job for Brogan the next time she saw him, *if* she saw him. Cautiously she called out, "Embry? Sarah?"

She cursed as she crashed through two large bushes, stumbled over the roots, and landed on her hands and knees. The metallic scent nearly choked her. Something wasn't right; she could feel it in her bones. Even her wolf tensed. Regretting her decision to leave the cabin, she edged forward. She'd crept only a few feet before she saw—him. The image slowly burned into her mind as she tried to absorb what she saw. Pine needles, no longer green but stained dark. A clump of trees, trails of dark-red lines and splatters. Her heart nearly stopped when she realized what she saw. Blood. *How can there be so much blood?*

Her legs trembled, but she forced herself to stand, unfortunately giving herself a perfect view. Past the trees, barely off the path. It took her mind a few minutes to process it. Blood. So much blood. A boot. Farther along, an arm. She didn't want to look, tried to force her eyes to close, but they wouldn't cooperate. She took two steps to the side, wanting nothing more than to run back to the safety of her cabin, lock the door, and never leave. She froze. In pine needles, surrounded by blood, eyes open, unblinking; they almost seemed to be watching her. She heard screams, bloodcurdling, unrelenting at first not realizing they were coming from her, as she stared at Embry's severed head.

Chapter Nine

B rogan shifted midair, bounding through the forest toward the sound, the blood pounding through his veins with such force he thought his heart would surely bust from his chest. One purpose, one thought raced through his mind. *Protect what's mine.* If anything happened to Gabby, if anyone dared to touch a hair on her beautiful head, he would kill them mercilessly.

His growl was savage as he felt another wolf at his side. In his current state, it took him a few seconds to recognize Ryker. Suddenly, the forest grew silent, and the screaming stopped, leaving behind a scent, heady, metallic...blood followed by putrid death.

When they approached the scene, both wolves skidded to a stop. Time stood still. Lava flowed through his veins. The past had come alive. Blood coated the ground, the trees. A body lay scattered in pieces across the forest floor, Magnum's favorite torture. Brogan's worst nightmare come to life. His Gabby. Her scent filled him as he felt his mind slipping away. Without her, he would go rogue. So much time wasted being apart at his choice. Again, he'd left her alone and unprotected. Again, he'd failed her.

Slowly, he padded across the forest floor. He hadn't bothered to shift back. He would stay the wolf until his death. A death he would gladly welcome as a world without Gabby would be one he'd have no desire to live in.

His head snapped toward the sound of retching. His heart swelled in his chest as he saw Gabby on her hands and knees, dry heaving. He bounded through the air. The second time his rear paws hit the ground, he shifted back to human as he reached her.

When he touched her, she cowered and rolled, screaming as she shifted. Crouched low, she backed up, horror shining in her eyes. Brogan took one step forward, raising his hands in peace as she growled. Despite his rage, he kept his voice calm. "Gabby. Baby, it's me. Shift back, honey. No one is going to hurt you."

Gabby met his next step forward by taking another back. He knew she had locked herself in her mind against the horror of what she saw. The sight of her so terrified made him want to kill something, someone, for making her hurt. He still managed to keep talking, soft, kind words. He wanted to howl in frustration as she stared back at him with fear in her eyes.

Ryker shifted and walked one step past him toward Gabby. Brogan tensed at his advance toward his mate. Ryker stopped and growled his order. "Shift. Back. Now."

With Drew out of commission, Ryker ruled. Gabby's wolf apparently recognized the power of the command. The shift wasn't as graceful or controlled as their normal way. Forcing a shift hurt like hell.

Brogan could only watch her small frame drop to the ground and shifted then curl into a tight ball. Brogan growled as he passed Ryker to get to his female. "Christ. You could have given her some time."

Ryker turned away. "There is no time. Take your female home. Stay with her. She needs you."

Brogan rushed to Gabby. Having no idea how long she had been here, what happened, or what she saw, he crouched beside her. His hands and eyes assessed her for any injuries. He thanked the gods he found none and pulled her into his arms, finally able to breathe.

Behind him he heard the enforcer's clipped voice, speaking on the phone, growling orders to the wolves and protectors to assist. Brogan still had Gabby pressed against him when Ryker returned.

"Gabby, what did you see?" Her body went rigid in his arms. She issued no response other than to shake her head to indicate negative. Crouching near them, the enforcer continued, "Gabby, I need words. What. Did. You. See?"

Her hands fisted, twisting Brogan's T-shirt, her body trembling against his. He wanted to kick Ryker's ass but couldn't, not only because the enforcer was now the wolf in charge, but they needed her answers. He stroked gently down her back. She cleared her throat, stuttered. "I-I-I only saw Embry. Nothing else, no one else here." Her body suddenly became rigid against his, her voice a whisper of a question, "Sarah?"

Ryker's expression never changed from calm resolve, his voice revealing no emotion. "Dead."

Brogan growled low. Ryker had never been known as Mr. Sensitive, but he could have softened the blow. "Christ."

At the first sob from Gabby, Ryker turned away, looking at the scene. "Do as I said. Take her home. Now."

In the distance, Brogan could hear the wolves coming to assist. He reached down and lifted Gabby to his chest, cradling her in his arms. He kept her face tucked against his chest. She had already seen enough. He walked her home as she cried.

Chapter Ten

Tears streamed down her face and wrenching sobs broke loose while Brogan carried her back to the cabin. She wanted to shift back into her wolf form and stay there. The wolf could handle what she'd seen better than the human. She would have shifted, it if it hadn't been for Brogan. The moment her muscles twitched to indicate the change, his lips pressed gently against her head, his voice a soothing whisper. "Stay with me, Gabby. I gotcha. Nothin' is going to happen to you now."

Slowly, her muscles relaxed. Brogan would keep her safe. She wasn't in danger at the moment. The issue was the visions of Embry he couldn't get out of her head. She hadn't asked about Sarah's death, didn't want to know how she'd been killed. She couldn't wrap her head around seeing what had happened to her friends, her neighbors. Now they were simply gone.

Lost in her own thoughts, she hadn't realized how far they had come until Brogan climbed the stairs to the cabin, opened the door, and carried her inside. His chest rose and fell with an exasperated sigh, one she knew came from the unlocked door. The door closed, and Brogan shifted her in his arms and clicked the lock into place. Muscles tensing to the point of cramping, she blew out a breath. She was not quite ready to be on her own. Brogan must have understood because, instead of putting her down, he adjusted her in his arms to toe off his boots.

Holding her close, he carried her into the bathroom and turned on the shower. She clutched at his shirt, hating feeling so weak. "Please don't leave me alone. I'm not ready yet."

He sat her on the counter, his strong hands moving to cup her face. "Baby, not leaving you. I am gonna get you cleaned up. Yeah?"

Her head rested against his chest as she whispered a relieved, "Okay."

Taking a step back, Brogan reached over his neck to grab his shirt and pull it off, then tossed it to the floor before he went to work on his jeans and socks as Gabby watched. Once he was naked, he helped her to stand then pulled her dress over her head and tossed it to join the rest of their clothes on the floor. After adding her panties to the pile, he guided her into the shower, her back to his front, one strong arm wrapped around her waist, holding her to him.

The cool water washed over her as strong hands began to move across her body gently washing away not only the dirt from the forest. She cleared her head and thought only of the moment. The heat from Brogan's body behind her. The feel of his hands. His scent surrounding her.

Unfortunately, the shower wouldn't last forever. Brogan washed himself quickly, reached out, turned off the water, then grabbed a towel from the rack. He wiped the droplets of water from her body and squeeze dried her hair before grabbing a dry towel to wrap around her body. Gabby stepped out to the sink, brushed her teeth then dropped the towel and snagged her fluffy white robe from the back of the door. Brogan dried himself off before he stepped back into his jeans, leaving the button undone, not bothering with the shirt. Her mouth went dry. Fully clothed, Brogan was hot; standing as he was now, he shot up the scale to volcanic.

At his chuckle, she started running a brush through her hair as the intimacy of it all hit her. She and Brogan sharing a bathroom. A twinge of sadness stabbed her in the heart. This was all she ever wanted with him. To be by his side, doing normal things mates did.

Suddenly, the brush disappeared from her hand, clattering as it hit the counter right before Brogan gathered her up in his arms. "Stop thinking. Let's get you something to eat then you need to sleep."

The mere thought of food caused her stomach to turn. "I don't think I'm ready for anything solid right now. Maybe a cup of tea. If you put me down, I can get it. There is some leftover stew I can heat up for you."

His eyes seemed to probe her, seeking answers to unasked questions before he carried her to the kitchen and placed her in a chair. "Tea and some toast; you gotta get something in there. You sit. I can handle myself."

Another twinge stung her heart as she watched Brogan move around her kitchen like he owned the place. Never once asking a question, finding everything he needed as if he'd cooked there a thousand times. She always kept water heating over the wood-burning stove. Brogan used the metal hook to open the cover, placing the wire toaster over the open flame, finally setting a small cast iron pan on top of the stove to warm. The kitchen was larger than in some of the other cabins she had been in. When she thought about it, same for the bathroom and shower. Nothing in the place was designed for a small woman to live alone. She'd never noticed before, but Brogan had designed the cabin to fit a man of his size.

He slid a cup of tea onto the table in front of her, the spicy aroma bringing her from her thoughts. She glanced up as Brogan moved away

"Never thought I would live to say it, but I can't stand when you're this quiet. Talk, Gabby. Not about today, unless you feel the need to."

She rose from the chair.

He glanced over his shoulder at her as he removed the toast and placed it on a plate in front of him. "Need somethin', babe?" He blocked her way as she started toward the cabinets.

"Just need some sugar for the tea."

"One spoonful, already in there. Sit. Eat." He pressed her back to her chair and placed the plate of toast in front of her. She looked down at it. Lightly toasted, heavily covered with wild raspberry jam. She spent days gathering berries and canning every year, selling off some but keeping plenty to get her through the winter.

When he sat down beside her with his stew and began to eat, he nodded. "You gonna eat it or stare at it."

"How did you know? The jam, the tea. We don't do this...this couple's thing."

"Babe. You do remember I used to live here all the time." She noticed how his face seemed to soften as he looked at her across the table. A look she always dreamed of. "Not a thing about you I don't remember. Even now, I come back, and the pack keeps me posted on what's going on. Like the jam everyone wants and swears you hoard like gold."

Gabby had to look away. With everything she had been through today, she wasn't sure if she was seeing things which simply weren't there. Her emotions were too raw. She sipped her tea and ate her toast as Brogan ate his stew. *Normal. Intimate.*

Finished eating, she started to rise from the chair to clear the table. Brogan reached across, grabbed the dishes, and set them in the sink. He returned to her side and placed a hand against the small of her back, guiding her out of the kitchen. "Bed."

Once they reached the bedroom, he reached down, flipped back the covers then grabbed her robe off her shoulders and tossed it on the small chair in the corner. She crawled into bed and curled beneath the blankets. Her gaze followed Brogan as he moved around the bed to the other side, dropped his jeans and climbed in beside her. Reaching out, he pulled her to his chest and wrapped her in his arms.

There she was again, lost in a dream she'd given up on a long time ago. She didn't move, only whispered into the darkened room, "Brogan, what are you doin' here? Not that I'm all fired up to be alone tonight. But all of this isn't exactly you."

"Doing what I should have done a long time ago. How about you let me take care of you, baby. Maybe this is the man I was supposed to be all along." His warm lips pressed against the top of her head.

With one beat, her heart lodged in her throat. She couldn't afford to think about Brogan being anything other than what he had always been. Her absent mate. She wanted to pull away from him, bury herself in the blankets, and hope they could shield her from him. She didn't. Instead, she stayed nestled in his warmth and strength. "Brogan, I don't think I can—"

"Sleep, Gabby. We don't need to talk about forever tonight. We don't need to talk about earlier today. You do need to know that when I heard you scream, smelled the blood, swear to fuck, Gabby, I have never been afraid of anything in my life. Today, I wasn't scared, I was fuckin' terrified. I brought you home and took care of you, not because you needed me to, but because I needed to do it. Exactly like right now, being with you here like this. I can feel your heart beating in your chest, the heat from your body pressed against mine. I know you're alive and safe. I need that, baby. You can give me that. Yeah?" His hand stroked gently across her skin the entire time he spoke, soothing her.

Not really trusting her voice, she let her body melt against his. Somehow, in the last day, they had journeyed into uncharted territory in their relationship. Not that she was complaining. Being with Brogan was all she ever wanted, but he still hadn't marked her. "Thank you. Yeah, Brogan, I can do that."

In bed, holding each other close, Gabby looked out into the darkness of the room. The day had been horrible, the worst in her life, but, at the moment, everything felt right. She tried to let the feeling soak through her. She felt warm, safe, content. But she still couldn't sleep. Instead, she lay quietly and staring at the ceiling, listening to the beat of Brogan's heart, his soft breaths. Apparently not well enough because Brogan squeezed her tight and whispered, "Sleep, Gabby, close your eyes."

"I can't do it. I can't close my eyes. If I do, all I see is Emb...." She couldn't hide the hitch in her voice as she spoke. "Make it go away, Brogan. Please. No matter how hard I try, I can't lie here and not think about it."

Chapter Eleven

Anything. Brogan would have done anything to never have seen the haunted look in her eyes as she looked up at him. Soft and sweet wasn't the way things happened between them. Every time he had taken her had been raw passion, primal need to possess her. He still felt the same desire, only now there was more. As much as she needed for him to erase her day, he needed to feel her alive.

He rolled her over, pressing soft, teasing kisses to her lips. "Open." Her lips parted, and his tongue swept inside, commanding the kiss. His hand smoothed over her hip, up over the soft skin of her stomach to palm her breast. He kissed a trail down her jaw, her neck, her chest. Her fingers went to his head, her nails scraping across his scalp. He loved the feel of her hands on him. Any way he could get them. Tonight wasn't about him; he planned on making it all about her. "Hands above your head, baby. No touching. Can you do that for me, or do I need to tie you?"

Heat flared in her eyes when he mentioned tying her up. Definitely something he would do to her in the future. He watched her move her hands above her head, grabbing the back of the pillow and holding on. "I think I can, except I like touching you."

Starting at her wrist, his finger traced down the muscles of her arm. He grinned as he saw the gooseflesh rise on her skin. "I like when you touch me, too, baby. You'll get your chance, but not tonight. Now, gimme that mouth."

He positioned himself over her, their mouths the only parts of their bodies touching. His tongue swept in, tasting, teasing, licking her lips until she arched toward him. He loved the way she responded to him. The room filled with the scent of her need. Gliding along her, he settled on his knees, between her legs, and watched her face as he cupped her breasts. He stroked one hardened nipple while he leaned down and took the other in his mouth. He swirling his tongue around the hardened berry, his teeth grazing it while he worked the other breast with his hand, pulling and twisting the nipple between his fingers. Her legs shifted against the sheets, and she raised her hips. Placing one final kiss on each breast, he kissed his way lower.

He spread her wide and lay between her legs. His cock was as hard as steel and twitched its approval as he looked at the glistening pink pussy. *His pussy.* He slid one finger through the drenched folds of skin, up to the swollen bud of her clit then down to the tight pucker of her ass. "One day, I'm gonna take you here, Gabby." He felt her body stiffen, and he moved his finger up to her cunt, drawing more of the juice down, slipping just the tip of his finger against her anus. He watched her face, her eyes fluttering at the most intimate penetration. "Yeah, baby, you'll like that. I'll make it good for you."

"Brogan, please, stop teasing me." Her legs writhed, and her hips pressed toward him.

"What do you want, Gabby? Tell me. You want my mouth or my cock?" He knew what she wanted, but he wanted to hear the dirty words from her sweet mouth before he gave in to her need.

She scowled down at him. "Mouth."

Yeah, he knew his girl loved his mouth. He turned his head, softly kissing the inside of her thigh. "This where you want my mouth? Gotta be a little more precise, baby. You want my mouth on your sweet pussy?"

He could feel the heat from her stare before he looked up at her. He did a piss poor job of hiding the grin that crossed his face. He turned his head, kissing the other thigh until she blurted out, "Pussy, Brogan. Now!"

He hooked her legs over his shoulders. "Love to hear you talk dirty, baby." He blew a stream of warm breath across her swollen clit and watched her entire body tremble then spread her wide with the tips of his fingers. "Nothing more beautiful." He slid his tongue between her folds, drinking down the evidence of her desire. Lapping at her swollen flesh, he pressed his tongue deep inside her tight channel and began fucking her. Her wetness covered his chin as he ate her as if he was starving. Which, when it came to her, he was. He might have just taken her yesterday, but all the years of denying what they had between them made him ravenous to take everything she had in every way. Her moans of pleasure became louder, more demanding. "Brogan, please, I need to come. Higher, touch me, dammit!"

He wanted to smile as he watched her face, a mask of desire and need, begging for what he could give her. All he could do was groan. As much as he had been teasing her, he had been teasing himself. His cock throbbed painfully, needing to be inside her. He gave her pussy one final lick from bottom to top, then rose over her. "Not coming without me, not this time."

He aligned the head of his dick with her tight channel and pressed in slowly. He used every ounce of his control not to slam root deep. Pure torture, pure ecstasy as he watched her body take him inside, inch by inch. When he sank in to the hilt, he froze for a moment, feeling her warmth wrapped around him. Capturing her mouth in a blistering kiss full of promise. "Watch me fuck you, Gabby. When you come, I want your eyes on me."

He growled low as he pulled out before sliding back in. He kept his rhythm slow and steady. He wasn't only fucking her. Today he would show her his love—a concept so foreign but so right. His Gabby. The words sounded perfect as they went through his mind. Beads of sweat began to roll down his back as he tried to hold off his release. Over and over, he pushed her to the edge, buried himself deep, and waited before starting again. The tingling sensation at the base of his spine told him time was up. "You're gonna come for me now, Gabby."

His strokes became faster, more powerful. He cocked his strokes to hit her clit with every thrust. He watched her gaze glaze over, her breaths coming in short pants. Her eyes and mouth opened wide, and he watched her reach it. Her body jerked with the force. "Brogan! Oh gods, Brogan!"

Her sex squeezed him like a vise, his own release stronger than anything he had ever felt. Their eyes never left each other as he continued to move inside her. He would swear they were looking at each other's souls. He let one of her legs fall from his shoulder as he leaned down, his canines elongated. Tilting her head to the side, he exposed her neck to him and struck deep into the crease of her neck and shoulder. The sweet taste of her blood filled his mouth, his hips jerked, her cunt squeezed him, and he came again.

Chapter Twelve

*B*ang! Bang! Bang! Gabby and Brogan both bolted up in the bed at the pounding on the door. Gabby felt as if her heart lodged in her chest. What could have happened now?

Brogan called out, "Hang on. I'm comin'."

Gabby jumped from the bed, even though Brogan nailed her with a look and snapped, "You keep your ass right where it is while I see who's here."

"It's my door they're knockin' on, so I would assume they're looking for me." Gabby grabbed her robe, pulled it on, and tied the sash of the belt as she followed him out to the living room. Brogan already had the front door open. Jaxon Boone and his human mate, Angeni Sweet, stood outside.

Jaxon tilted his chin in greeting, his eyes darting between the two, an amused grin pulling at the corners of his mouth. "Ryker called a meeting. He needs everyone in town now."

Brogan asked in a low voice. "They find anything from yesterday?"

Gabby paused next to him. "You don't have to whisper. I'm right here, and I can still hear you. Not to mention I'm wolf. You could close the door and stand on the porch and I would still know what you were saying."

She had tried for the brave front, still shaky, but she felt better. She sighed. "I promise I'm not going to fall apart." At least she hoped she wouldn't. She would never in her life forget what she saw yesterday. She could become the scared mouse and hide in her cabin or harden her heart, refusing to let anyone in so she never again felt loss. Neither option was acceptable. She couldn't let the tragedy she'd witnessed change her.

Brogan reached out and pulled her to his side, wrapping his arm around her waist and tucking her against his side in a move both possessive and protective. Jaxon's lips curled in a knowing smirk. He studied her, probably to see if she was in fact going to fall apart then looked at Brogan before he continued. "Don't know a whole hell of a lot. Everyone's talkin', but Ryker hasn't said anything for certain. You know how pack gossip goes. Don't believe anything until you hear it from the alpha's mouth. Probably what the big meeting is about. You two come together. No going anywhere alone."

Brogan stiffened. "No worries there. After yesterday, this is about as alone as Gabby is going to be until this the bastard is caught."

Jaxon slung his arm over Angeni's shoulder and tucked her against his side. Wolves, in general, liked to play the possessive game when it came to their females. Turn the male wolf into a mate and it kicked up to a level to not only dangerous but deadly.

A soft smile crossed Angeni's face before she reached out and took Gabby's hand. "I don't get a lot of visions here in Los Lobos." She laughed softly.

Jaxon muttered, "Thank the gods," under his

breath.

Angeni rolled her eyes. "As I was going to say, I'm not complaining. I enjoy the peace and quiet Los Lobos has to offer. I have to tell you, though, you've always been surrounded by a hint of a blue aura, a kind of sadness. You can fool some people in town, but not usually me. There is a change now." Angeni looked between her and Brogan. "Yellow surrounds you, happiness, real, honest happiness. I need to say, it looks great on you. Whatever your worries are, things are going to be just fine."

Gabby smiled at her then up at Brogan, wrapping an arm around his waist as he did the same to her. "Yeah, they are."

Jaxon's hold on Angeni tightened then loosened as she began to talk. Gabby knew their story. The pack history was filled with the horrors of Magnum's reign of terror. Few who'd remained during that time hadn't suffered in some way, Jaxon included. He hadn't believed in anything when he first met Angeni. He definitely hadn't believed in her gifts as a seer. At least not until he'd seen them firsthand. Town gossip had claimed Angeni had been possessed by Magnum, who wanted revenge against Drew for his death. Jaxon's ability to find faith and trust help them discover love.

With another slight grin, Jaxon winked. "You finally took the plunge, man. When all of this shit is over, there will be a double reason to celebrate."

Brogan shrugged. "I figure I'm in for enough teasing. Let's pass on it for now. We'll get dressed and meet up in town."

Closing the door, Brogan released Gabby and turned her toward the bedroom. "Get dressed. I wanna hear what Ryker has to say before he talks to the pack. The way things are going down, I don't think it is in the best interest of anyone to keep him waiting for very long."

Gabby hurried into the bedroom, released the sash, and let her robe fall to the floor in front of the closet. For the first time, she felt nervous about going into town. Normally, she would be the one sitting in the middle of Gee's bar, sipping on soda and catching up on all the latest gossip. With people getting murdered and her accidentally coming upon the scene, she wasn't in a big hurry to get there. She'd told Ryker she hadn't seen anything else. What she had seen had been more than enough for her. If she never had to think or talk about it again, it would be more than fine.

She selected another peasant dress from her closet. Once dressed, she searched for her flip-flops. Confused at first, it took her a moment to remember she'd worn them the day before. She must have lost them while running through the forest. Heaviness started to settle into her chest at the memories. The forest could have them. No way she would go in search of them. Quickly, she tried to banish thoughts of yesterday. She would get a new pair of shoes the next time she went into town. She selected her Chucks from the bottom of the closet, moved to the side of the bed, and sat down while putting them on. She felt Brogan's eyes on her, one brow raised in question. He had pulled the black T-shirt over his head, opened the fly of his jeans, and tucked it in. "You forgetting something? Panties?"

Her smile was one of innocence. "Laundry is my least favorite thing. You seem to be doing the commando thing yourself."

"God help me. You may have to take notes

during this meeting. I'm not sure if I'm going to be able to think about anything other than you naked under that dress."

"Wait, I thought you knew everything about me."

"Babe, if anyone in town had told me you run around in a dress with no panties, I probably would've killed them."

She giggled as she finished tying her shoes, jumped up, and grabbed the brush from the bathroom. She brushed through the tangles then tied her hair in a high ponytail.

Brogan called from the living room, "Get a move on." She walked in just in time to see Brogan grab the key from the table by the door and slide it into his pocket.

She went through the door, started down the steps, and froze, listening to the sounds of the forest. The rustle of leaves, birds singing, and squirrels barking. All things seemed to be as they were when she left yesterday. A mere touch of his hand on her shoulder and she nearly jumped her out of her skin. Strong hands cupped her cheeks, one sliding around to the back of her neck, controlling her as if he could feel her need to run. He tilted his head, studying her expression. "You good? Nothin' out here is gonna hurt you, Gabby. I won't let it."

He was right, and she knew it. "Yeah, I'm good. I was thinking about when I left here yesterday, and I guess it got to me a bit. Come on, we'd better go."

Warm lips pressed against her forehead, lingering a bit, his warmth settling into her. Relaxing his embrace, he laced their fingers together then led her down the path. The only tense moment came as they passed Embry and Sarah's cabin. A heaviness settled back into her chest at the thought of never seeing them there again. Brogan quickened their pace as they went past it. She found it unbelievable how in tune he was with her emotions, which seemed to be swinging every direction within minutes. "How about, when we catch this guy and it's over, I take you away for a week? Head into town? I'll spring for one of the fancy hotels with a big tub."

"You don't need to do anything special. I know you're trying to get my mind off things, but I'm really okay. I'm not made of glass."

"Believe me, I know you're not. You're one of the strongest females I know. Plus, who said anything about getting your mind off things. I'm just trying to get you naked in a hot bath in a hotel with you all to myself." When she looked up at him, she saw the wicked grin and watched him waggle his brows. There was no stopping the laughter at his expression. "Good gods, the beast has awakened."

He dropped her hand, reached behind her, and cupped her backside, fisting the material of her dress and gathering it in her hand. She swatted him and pulled away, still laughing. A new side of Brogan she had never seen before, playful and sweet. Sure, she knew his mind would be in the woods, tracking the murderer, doing what he could for the pack, but he taking time to care for her, too. He caught up with her before they hit the dirt road leading into town. Up ahead she could see the old barn and members of the pack gathering. She took a deep breath and released it slowly as they walked through town.

The closer they got to the barn, the thicker the tension in the air became until it was pulsing through the air. Brogan kept a tight grip on her hand as he weaved them through the crowd to reach Ryker, who stood on a raised platform against the back wall.

Clay, Danni, and Thane were at Ryker's side. Each gave Gabby a cursory once-over. Brogan moved behind her, his arms dropping over her shoulders, wasting no time letting everyone know exactly the status of their relationship. No discussion. They were together, and everyone would know it.

He dove right into the reason they were there. "Any news? I didn't get to spend a lot of time at the scenes yesterday. I saw enough to say, with the way Sarah was laid out, it was almost like she was cherished and the killer showed regret. Embry, that scene I would describe as complete and total rage. I don't believe any of us is missing the fact that in both cases the females were humans, both were mated. While I think everyone needs to be watching their backs, if you have a human mate, take extra care. I don't think I would be letting her outta my sight."

Thane filled them in on the situation with Charles. He had been cleared as a suspect. Apparently he had been whacked in the back of the head, knocked out cold, and had the gash to prove it. When he came to and saw Sonya dead, he lost it, went feral, and took off. After hearing Gabby's screams yesterday, the feral feeling hit a little too close to home. "Looks like we're back to square one then. Searching for a fuckin' ghost."

Ryker tipped his chin to acknowledge the statement. Brogan tried to get a read on the man, but his emotions were locked down tight. Saja, Ryker's mate, was human. The fact that the two women killed were human had to be messing with his mind.

Ryker took a step forward. The crowd fell silent. "Everyone, home. There will be no leaving for any reason, and no one will be permitted to leave town.

Anyone caught outside will be dealt with swiftly. If you need something from town, get it now. You have one hour to be home. I suggest you leave now."

There were few murmurs from the crowd, but no one spoke directly. Ryker had issued martial law on the pack. The members quickly dispersed.

Brogan and Gabby stopped at Brogan's truck to grab his duffel bag as they left town. Brogan focused on keeping Gabby safe and returning to the trail. Thoughts of Charles consumed him. The male would never be the same. At the cabin, he unlocked the door and pulled her inside.

Inside the cabin, he let primal need take over. Closing the door behind him, he tossed his duffel bag toward the bedroom and pushed her against the door. His lips crashed down on hers. Tilting his head, he licked at the seam of her lips until they parted. He growled as he slid his tongue inside at the first taste.

He wrapped her ponytail around one hand while the other palmed her breast through the thin cotton dress. She clutched his shoulders, pulling him to her. He separated from her long enough to grab the dress by the hem and lift it up and off, tossing it away. In a split second, he was back on her, his mouth at her breast, his tongue lapping at her hardened nipple before sucking it hard into his mouth. He forced her to spread with his foot. The scent of her arousal surrounded him as he slid two fingers through the folds of her labia. "Fuck. Thank the gods for dirty laundry. So damn wet. Ready for me. I need to be inside you."

Her body shivered in response. He thumbed her clit. "Get there, Gabby. I need to fuck you."

She rode his fingers, her panting breaths and soft moans growing louder until she finally screamed,

"Brogan! Oh. My. God!"

She came apart in his arms, his mouth capturing her cries of pleasure as he reached between them, quickly unbuttoning his jeans, sliding down the zipper down and lowering his jeans on his hips. While she still trembled, he moved his hands to cup her ass, lifting her, her legs wrapping around his waist as he pressed her against the door. He entered her in one stroke, burying himself balls deep. He growled at the feel of her tight cunt quivering around his cock. He began to move, taking her hard, his hips pistoning into her wet heat. He moved his hands to her hips, guiding her movements, slamming her down onto his rigid cock. Everything in the world ceased to exist. Only Gabby in his arms, his cock fitting inside her perfectly, the sounds of her passionate cries, his own grunts of need.

He arched his hips, hammering deeper inside, hitting the special spot he knew would push her over the edge. "Come with me, Gabby, now, baby, let go. I gotcha."

Three strokes and her body stiffened for a second before she flew apart in his arms. He barely felt the tingles begin and his balls tighten against him before his release shot through him. He continued to hammer into her, sinking deep then freezing, his hips jerking as her sweet cunt squeezed out every drop of his seed inside her. His canines elongated, and her head tipped to the side offering herself. Without a question in his mind, he licked the sweet spot at the base of her neck and shoulder. A low, possessive growl escaped as he sank his fangs deep into his mark. *Mine.*

Her head rested against his chest, and his arms held her tight as they both came down. His cock glided slowly inside her. He was in no hurry to lose the connection between them. Unfortunately, he had things to take care of, most importantly a murderer to track down. As soon as he could, he planned on taking an entire day, maybe a week, and keeping her in his bed.

He carried her into the bathroom, sat her ass on the counter, and cleaned her up. She laughed softly, a blush coloring her cheeks. "You do know you don't have to do that."

He wiped gently with the washcloth, leaning down, his lips hovering over hers. "Who do you belong to? Whose sweet pussy is this?"

He watched her face soften. "Everything I have belongs to you."

"Damn right, and I take care of what's mine." He kissed her again after he finished cleaning them both up. Taking her at the door should have at least dimmed his need to have her, but, with the taste of her lips, his cock grew hard. He had to force himself away. Lifting her off the counter, swatting her ass, he pushed her toward the door to the bedroom and said, "Put on some clothes and make me some coffee before I need to head out."

She gave him a wicked smile over her shoulder as she left. He watched her bare ass until she disappeared from sight. His palm ached to spank her sweet ass, watch it turn red under his touch. There would be plenty of time later.

He grabbed some clean clothes from his duffel and finished dressing. Coffee was already done when he met her in the kitchen. He took the cup in one hand, her hand in his other. He led her through the cabin, letting her go before he opened the door and they walked out onto the porch. He thought of Sarah and Embry on their porch only yesterday. Their position, Brogan behind Gabby as she stood by the railing, was exactly the same. Now, Sarah and Embry were both dead.

Brogan leaned down, kissing Gabby's neck. "You know, when I leave you, lock the door. Do not go outside for any reason. Not even to stand on the porch. I'll be back to check on you as often as I can or I'll have one of the others stop by. You don't open the door for anyone but Thane, Clay, or Ryker, get me?"

"Yeah, I get you. Believe me, I have no plans to go anywhere." She leaned back, giving him her weight. "I love you, Brogan."

"Love you too, baby." His lips lingered on her neck, his tongue lapping at his mark on her flesh. An odd comfort rose inside him as he stroked the skin. Gabby's entire body tensed in his arms, the fine hairs over his body standing on end, their moment broken when blood-curdling screams in the distance rent the air.

About the Author

Cam Cassidy is an erotic romance author, her current with with a paranormal sizzle. She spent her life growing up in a small Ohio farming community. The lack of neighbors and companionship of mostly cows and horses in her youth left her plenty of time for her passion of reading to flourish.

As an adult, Cam is married and the mother of three ornery children who keep her on her toes. The cup of coffee in her hand is a trademark. She works full time in the medical field. In her spare time, she spends every minute reading and writing. Watching her children ride horses, dirt bikes with a notebook in hand to never miss jotting down that next all important story idea.

All of the "hard work" reading and writing sitting beside the fire drinking a glass of wine. Or was it between loads of laundry? Her dream of becoming a published author have come true.

Also by Cam Cassidy

A Wolf Awakens